The Pen Pieyu Adventures

Sir Princess Petra's

Mission

The Pen Pieyu Adventures

Sir Princess Petra's
Mission

Book Three

Diane Mae Robinson

First published in 2015 by Tate Publishing & Enterprises, LLC
Second edition published by Diane Mae Robinson Ink, March 23, 2017

Illustrations by Michael Bermundo

Published in Canada

ISBN: 978-0-9952482-9-8
·1. Juvenile Fiction / Readers / Chapter Books
·2. Juvenile Fiction / Action & Adventure / General
16.3.17

Dedication

For Norman, Darrin, Mabel, and Willy.
The angels who watch over me
from the gardens of heaven

Praise for *Sir Princess Petra: The Pen Pieyu Adventures, Book 1*

Her writing grabs you, is perfectly pitched, nuanced, a fresh approach.

—Lieutenant Governor of Alberta
Emerging Artist Award adjudicators

The Pen Pieyu Adventures: Sir Princess Petra is a maverick fantasy, packed with plot twists and turns, unexpected obstacles and problems, and brilliant flashes of humor and originality. *Sir Princess Petra* charms and entrances the reader.

—Midwest Book Review

Sir Princess Petra is an empowering, delightfully imaginative story. Petra's character is both confident and charismatic. I highly recommend *Sir Princess Petra* for school, public, and personal library collections.

—University of Manitoba Reviews

This is a great book for elementary schools and public libraries. I would highly recommend this book.

—Brenda Ballard for Readers' Favorite

Praise for *Sir Princess Petra's Talent: The Pen Pieyu Adventures, Book 2*

I love this book series! *Sir Princess Petra's Talent* is a wonderful, fast-paced story full of humor and profound messages—what a powerful combination!
—Alinka Rutkowska, award winning children's author

Diane Mae Robinson's second book in *The Pen Pieyu Adventures* series is a delightful read and one that is sure to engage and enthrall young readers.
   —Children's Literary Classics Int'l Book Awards

A fairy tale enriched with magical worlds. The book that we want to define as a graceful masterpiece in children's literature.
                              —Advices Books

Diane Mae Robinson's fantasy adventure tale, *Sir Princess Petra's Talent*, is quite simply wonderful.
              —Jack Magnus for Readers' Favorite

Praise for *Sir Princess Petra's Mission: The Pen Pieyu Adventures, Book 3*

The degree of imagination is matched by the terrific humor and sense of fun. From the beginning chapter to the end, this book is a treasure and one that is highly recommended.

—Grady Harp, Top 100 Amazon Reviewer

The third title in author Diane Mae Robinson's outstanding *The Pen Pieyu Adventures* series is an impressive and thoroughly entertaining read and very highly recommended.

—Midwest Book Review

An enchanting book, filled with wry humor and titillating prose, sort of Dr. Seuss without the rhyme.

—Charles A. Ray, author

More reviews for *The Pen Pieyu Adventures* series: https://www.dragonsbook.com

Awards for *Sir Princess Petra: The Pen Pieyu Adventures, Book 1*

2012 Lieutenant Governor of Alberta Emerging Artist Award (literary arts)
2012 Purple Dragonfly Book Award
2013 Readers' Favorite International Book Award
2014 Sharp Writ Book Award

Awards for *Sir Princess Petra's Talent: The Pen Pieyu Adventures, Book 2*

2014 Readers' Favorite International Book Award
2015 Children's Literary Classics Seal of Approval
2015 Children's Literary Classics Book Award
2015 Los Angeles Book Festival Book Award
2015 Purple Dragonfly Book Award

Awards for *Sir Princess Petra's Mission: The Pen Pieyu Adventures, Book 3*

2016 Readers' Favorite International Book Award
2016 Book Excellence Award

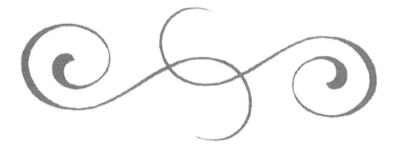

MAP OF
PEN PIEYU KINGDOM
AND SURROUNDING LANDS

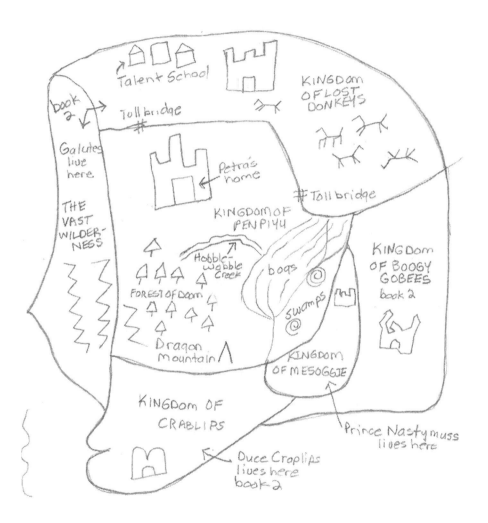

Talent School

Toll bridge

book 2

Galutea live here.

THE VAST WILDER-NESS

KINGDOM OF LOST DONKEYS

Petra's home

Toll bridge

KINGDOM OF PEN PIYU

Hobble-Wobble Creek

bogs

KINGDOM OF BOOGY GOBEES book 2

FOREST OF DOOM

swamps

Dragon Mountain

KINGDOM OF MESOGGIE

KINGDOM OF CRABLIPS

Prince Nastymuss lives here

Duce Croplips lives here book 2

Diane Mae Robinson

Synopsis of Book One

At Longstride Castle, in the Kingdom of Pen Pieyu, it is Princess Petra's ninth and royal birthday. Her father, King Longstride, has promised her anything her heart desires. Petra chooses to become a royal knight and protect her kingdom. (Thus far, Longstride Castle has no knights as all the silly soldiers are still trying to become knights.)

After much commotion in the royal throne room, King Longstride has no choice but to grant her request. The royal rule book says nothing about a girl becoming a knight but only that the proposed knight must perform a deed from a list of three. The choices are: to capture a crocodile and make his skin into a royal leather chair; to hush the howling, nasty dragon, Snarls, in the Forest of Doom; or to eat a roomful of raw onions. Petra chooses to hush the howling, nasty dragon, Snarls.

Outfitted in the best royal pots and pans, Petra heads off into the Forest of Doom with nothing more than her cake-knife sword and a sack of onions to search out the dragon. After a few strange encounters in the Forest of Doom, Petra finally confronts Snarls, and after some onion-throwing and eyebrow-singeing, she discovers not all is as it seems. Snarls is howling because his tail is stuck under a pile of fallen rocks, not because he is mean and nasty. Petra helps Snarls escape his predicament, and the two become fast friends.

Petra returns to the castle to announce her accomplishment of hushing the howling dragon and, thus, gains her real armour. Thereafter, she is forever known as Sir Princess Petra.

Of course, Petra and Snarls go on to have more adventures and encounter other zany characters: Bograt, the bog witch; Prince Nastybun and his midget army; and Letgo, the crocodile. And Pen Pieyu Kingdom will never be the same.

Synopsis Of Book Two

King Longstride has written a new rule in the royal rule book that declares all Princess Knights of Kingdom Pen Pieyu (Petra is still the only knight in the lands of Pen Pieyu) must attend Talent School and acquire a princess talent certificate or suffer the consequences of the royal magician's spell to be turned into a frog to live in the bogs for five years.

Of course, the king writes these rules to deter Petra from her silly knight nonsense and act more like a princess. And of course, Petra wants no part of being a girly princess.

But when Petra believes that the royal magician has turned all nine of the palace soldiers into frogs she, reluctantly, agrees to go.

Petra and Snarls (the dragon who is now her royal steed and co-adventurer, and also the head chef at Longstride Castle) head off for the Land of Lost Donkeys, where King Asterman awaits her arrival at Talent School.

En route to Talent School, the adventurers meet a very strange knight named Prince Duce Crablips from the Kingdom of Crablips who declares a duel with Petra.

Okay, so the dueling thing was all over a silly misunderstanding, but once they straighten that all out (and only one small injury is sustained by Snarls), Petra and Duce become friends and the trio all head off to Talent School.

Snarls joins Barbeque School. Duce decides on Crochet School. And Petra is left to choose amongst some very undesirable schools: Princess Etiquette School, Knitting School, Cloak Sewing School, Get Over Fainting Fast School, Jewelry Budgeting School, Preparing to Be Engaged School. There is, however, one quite intriguing school that, due to a technical error on King Asterman's part, does not have the proper Closed sign posted.

Well, Petra does choose a Talent School, and she does a pretty good job of it by using her very good imagination and, hence, attaining a talent certificate. But her new talent is not quite what the king had in mind for his princess daughter.

After Snarls pulls a somewhat klutzy manoeuvre in Barbeque School, the trio has to skedaddle—Talent School is definitely over.

On their way back to Pen Pieyu, Petra spots a dilapidated sign on a tree—a sign with warnings posted by the ganutes of the Vast Wilderness. Realizing they are upon the borders of the Vast Wilderness (where no adventurer has ventured before), Petra decides they should explore.

The ganutes have an attack first questions later strategy. Once this chaos is all sorted out, somehow, this all leads to someone else becoming a knight.

Back at Longstride Castle, Petra announces her new talent, introduces a bunch of ganutes for potential knights, and declares the newest knight of Pen Pieyu—all of this being a very big shock to the king and queen.

But Petra has a way of smoothing things over. She shares her new talent with the kingdom at the newest knight's knighting party.

All is well in the Kingdom of Pen Pieyu. And Pen Pieyu Kingdom will never, ever be the same.

CHAPTER 1

THE ROYAL SEAL-OF-APPROVAL MISSION

Petra awoke to the sound of the royal councilman's bugle, again. She hastily dressed in leggings and tunic still damp from her friendly sundown-wrestling match with Letgo, the crocodile, and scurried down to the royal throne room.

The royal councilman was whirling around in his manic flurry of the third early-morning summoning event in six full moons. He located the royal rule book under the queen's throne, touched it like it was on fire, hastened to open it to page 111, then skidded the open book on the stone floor to land up near the king's feet. The king gave him a royal-councilmen-are-a-shilling-a-dozen glare.

"Father, Mother, you summoned me?" Petra rolled her eyes when she noticed the rule book was even thicker than last she saw it.

"Yes, my dear princess," the king said with an amused grin, running his finger down the page to find the spot.

Petra sighed.

The king spoke loud as he read out, "It is hereby written that all certified Princess Knights—meaning you—must accomplish the hereby-stated royal seal-of-approval mission before the next two moondowns.

Hence if the hereby-said should fail this royal seal-of-approval mission, which is of the utmost importance to the well-being of the shareholders of Kingdom Pen Pieyu—meaning me and the queen—the hereby-said Princess Knight will henceforth be required to relinquishment of the hereby-noted knighthood to the full completeness so as to render it none and never was. Also, by fail, forfeit, or giving up on this mission, the certified Princess Knight will henceforth deem the by-default bog witch's knighthood—meaning Bograt —null, none, and never was." The king gave the page a quizzical look, mumbled for a time, then raised his head and broke out his half-moon grin while taking up the confused queen's hand in his.

Petra crossed her arms and gave him her best I-hate-that-royal-rule-book stare with her right eye, while her left eyebrow rose to convey the it-doesn't-even-make-sense arch.

"Silence!" the king ordered and continued to read, louder this time, "The hereby-said certified Princess

Knight's mission will be to venture into the unventured land of the Boogy Gobees, alone, and capture the first notorious-fabled car-panther she encounters and henceforth, whereupon a successful mission, deliver the first notorious-fabled car-panther creature she encounters to the Kingdom of Pen Pieyu."

Petra felt like streams of steam were about to sizzle out of her ears. "That's the most ridiculous rule yet—it is poorly written, does not make complete sense, and also, you just recently made it up. There has never been a certified Princess Knight before me and previous to six new moons ago, nor a by-default bog witch knight before Bograt and previous to three new moons ago. Besides that, what or who is a car-panther? And what exactly do you mean: go *alone* to capture a car-panther?"

Just then, Snarls entered the royal throne room with a shiny silver tray of steaming teas and aromatic pine nut crumpets. Startled by Petra's last words, he dropped the tray and heaved out a misguided fire breath that grazed the top of the queen's bouffant hair.

"Car-panthers are vicious scallywags, said to have saw-blade teeth, stiffened with iron on the tips for good measure," Bograt stated as she sauntered into the room. "Cut the moat bridge right in half and kings with bad grammar into fours." She gave a wink toward Petra.

"Stop that nonsense jabber at once!" the king shouted while still bopping at the queen's head. Finally succeeding to make for her a much smaller smoldering hairdo, he continued, "*Alone*—it means by oneself, no other person, et cetera, et cetera."

Petra marched over to the royal rule book, flipped back to page 101, and traced her finger along the words until she found the segment she was looking for. "Well, Father, this particular rule, written by you several full moons prior, states: 'All knights may choose their own steed. All steeds will willingly accompany their knights. All knights will stick together.' And it has the royal seal of approval, which, of course, means you sealed it yourself and your new rule cannot alter a previous sealed rule."

The king's bottom lip sagged and twitched and looked like it might fall off. The royal councilman's eye's flashed open wide; he turned and ran.

As the king paced, he tugged at his grey beard, then stopped doing both and narrowed his eyes to glare his why-you-little-sneaky-princess glare at Petra. "How did you know exactly what page that rule was on? And how did you know you would have to find it? Have you been reading in the royal rule book without my knowledge? Have you been in my library?"

"Father, your library does not have a Private sign on the door. Anybody in the kingdom can go in there. That royal-sealed rule is in the royal rule book too, page 9," Petra answered with a wink to Snarls, who was now standing close by her side, fidgeting and fiddling with his claws.

By this time, the queen had finally located her pocket mirror from somewhere in the tremendous folds of her gown, looked into it, screamed, and promptly fainted. The king plopped back into his chair, rubbed his scrunched-up face for a time before he raised his arms up in the air.

Petra already knew that meant, "you are absolutely quite right, my dear daughter." She gave Snarls and Bograt the let's-get-going signal with her thumb. Snarls scurried after her; Bograt went the other direction.

"You still have to do the mission part, you know," the king called out after her.

CHAPTER 2

A MISFORTUNATE EVENT

"Snarls, after all your prior fuss, you do appear to becoming fond of your pink saddle." Petra smiled while the armoury guard presented her armour, which she refused.

"It does grow on one. Kind of a new-age steed fashion statement, don't you think?" Snarls twisted back and forth to make the tassels swing.

Bograt burst through the armoury doors, lugging two huge sacks of onions over her shoulders. "And just who is going to guard the royal onion room while I'm away? Those onion-sucking nitwit soldiers will have the whole onion room devoured by next moondown."

"Oh, Bograt, don't fret so. The royal councilman has been stashing that room with onions for years. It will never be bare. Why do you think nobody has ever accomplished the royal deed listed in the royal rule book of eating a roomful of onions to become a knight?"

Bograt grinned a show of pointy teeth. "Ha! Good one."

Petra motioned Bograt to jump up behind her on Snarls' back.

"No way. Not riding on anything with four legs that wears a sissy pink saddle. Besides, need to be prepared—there could be vicious, notorious-fabled, dragon-eating car-panthers lurking about that sense our mission and are already stalking us."

Snarls gasped and snorted out a fiery blitz of sparks. The armoury guard ducked just in time. "Okay, why has nobody explained to me before that these are notorious-fabled, dragon-eating car-panthers?"

"Bograt, stop that! She's making it up, Snarls. Nobody knows what a car-panther is, including my father. They may not even be real, probably fantasy fairytale stuff. Or maybe they are something like the ganutes. Discovering the ganutes in the Vast Wilderness was only scary before we found out what they were really like, remember?" Petra frowned her eyebrows at Bograt, who whistled and dawdled behind them.

After a long spell of wordless journey, the trio came upon the edge of Hobble-Wobble Creek. Bograt plunged right into the creek; Snarls hesitated, watching swirls in the water.

"It's okay, Snarls. It's just Letgo, the crocodile, and her youngins. I told you before, they are friends."

"Puhhh, I am somewhat and then fairly sure the palace soldiers named her Letgo for a good reason when they were trying out for the knight deed of making her skin into a new leather chair for the king." Snarls cocked his head to the left, let loose three quick puffs of smoke, then dipped a tiny piece of claw into the creek, which he instantly pulled back out. Petra rubbed her hand over the highly-polished scales of his neck, and soon, with tip-claw steps, he entered the murky water.

Huge bumpy eyes attached closely to a gigantic opened jaw lunged out right in front of Snarls' sniffing nose. Snarls jumped, straight up and a good length out of the water, landing back in the creek in a scrunched-up position with his legs tucked under him. His dragon belly flop sent all the water around him hurling into huge waves. Petra was washed off the slippery saddle, and just as a wave tried to claim her, Snarls grabbed the back of her pants with his front teeth and skedaddled to the other shore. Meanwhile, Bograt rode a wave to disappear around the bend. A fading "Weeeee"echoed after her.

CHAPTER 3

THE SWAMP ENCOUNTER

"Great, now we've lost Bograt." Petra dumped the water and weeds and mud out of her boots; a tiny sardine washed out and wiggled on the ground. She picked up the fish by the tail and placed it back into the water.

"Okay, it wasn't my fault," Snarls snapped. "You said Letgo was friendly."

"Letgo is friendly. She was just saying hello, and she likes to peck my cheek in the mornings. Sheesh, Snarls!"

"Oh yeah? Well…oops. Um, there's something else too." Snarls flashed a fake grin. "You have a hole in the seat of your pants, you know, where I saved you.

Petra twisted around to look at her backside and rolled her eyes. "Thanks. For saving me, I mean." Thinking about what to do next, Petra put on her helmet with the now limp pink plume and slipped her boots back on. "We're going to have to go on without Bograt. We don't have time to look for her and carry out the mission before two moondowns. Bograt will be just fine on her own. She's a very independent bog witch, and she'll surely show up somewhere unexpected." Petra bit on her lip for a moment.

"That's what we'll do, Snarls. Hurry up, and let's get going."

"Hey, you're the certified Princess Knight. You're the main lady. I'm just the certified royal supreme chef and dutiful royal steed, right? What do I know about decision making? Hey, my resume is soaked."

"Why do you have . . . oh never mind. Yes, dear royal steed, I should have asked. Please, tell me your professional steedly, chefy opinion."

"Hmmm, well, actually, my opinion is exactly the same as yours now that I've had time to think about it," Snarls huffed. "And since you nearly asked, I always carry my resume, in case of and perchance we come across another kingdom where the chefs require my expertise on chefy matters. By the way, you do know that Bograt has all the onions, right? The *onions* you always carry on your knight missions, your knight *weapon* of choice?"

Petra swung back into the saddle and gave Snarls a little jab to the ribs with her heels.

No words were exchanged between them all the while

Snarls sloshed through the soggy moss of the bogs.

~~~~~~~~~~~~~~~~~~~~~

Before long, they were at the deeper swamps where Snarls started bellyaching about how horrible the goopy mud felt between his toes. He purposely swung his feet higher, flinging up more mud and gunk that flew upward before splattering Petra, then himself. Petra wiped mud from her eyes as she surveyed the land. Something seemed amiss. The swamps were scattered with severely misshapen trees; long-time-dead-looking brittle trees that somehow still stood upright. Muck of a dingy green hue floated in lumpy patches atop the foul water and reminded her of dead rotting frogs. Although she had never been this far east of Pen Pieyu and although she tried to convince herself that perhaps all swamps looked like this, still she felt that on guard, prickly feeling on the back of her neck. She squeezed her legs tighter to Snarls' sides.

Suddenly Snarls froze in his tracks—his body still lurching forward for a moment before springing back to where his feet were. Petra nearly flew over Snarls' head and grabbed on to his ears to gain her balance.

"What! What's the matter?"

"I'm stuck. I can't pick up my feet. Ewwww. It's like I'm glued to the bottom of a porridge pot," Snarls squealed out.

An outcry screeched through the air, coming from up ahead and to their left, "Get the giant! We'll capture the monster!" Sticky-sounding, sloshing footsteps belonging to miniature, mud-covered knights charged a sortie to surround Petra and Snarls like some dark magic. A bombardment of tiny arrows let loose from behind. Petra winced as an arrow struck her hand. She pulled it out with the other hand and threw it into the mire.

"Halt this nonsense ambush at once! I am Sir Princess Petra of Kingdom Pen Pieyu," Petra shouted, but her voice didn't sound her own. She hollered in a lower tone, with more force, "I am on a knight's mission—"

"Cease fire!" the miniature knight commander ordered as he held up his arm. He took off his helmet. "Umm, Petra, is that really you?"

Petra swiped at her eyes, clearing away the excess mud that still clung to her eyelashes and clouded her vision somewhat. "Well, if it isn't Prince Norton Nastybun and the puny army from Kingdom Mesoggie. You have stabbed my hand and severely altered my good nature. What in all the entire kingdoms are you doing here?"

"Sorry, sorry, I didn't know it was you, Petra. Honest, honest," Norton sputtered out in his squeaky violin voice. "You are very near the Lands of Mesoggie. We guard the swamps here. Aw, Petra, are you going to tell your father? You know he will make us wear frilly dresses for interfering in a knight's mission if you do."

Petra couldn't help but laugh—it was the one and only good rule her father had ever made. "It shall be pardoned, Norton. It was all just a big misunderstanding."

"Yeah, easy for you to say," Snarls grumbled. "Could somebody get these misunderstandings out of my backside?"

The puny army climbed on top of one another to form a puny army ladder, and the last puny knight up proceeded to remove the arrows from Snarls' rump.

"Ouch, ouch, ouch. Aaah, ouch!" Snarls yelped before two wayward fireballs escaped his nostrils to torch the top tips of Prince Nastybun's curls. "Oops."

Norton's hair smoldered while he helped Petra down from Snarls' back. With clumsy effort, he guided her to more solid ground, then turned and gave another order, "Puny army, help get that dragon unstuck. Meet us back at the castle for some merriment and cheer, but not until you get the *dragon* cleaned up."

"You know my name is Snarls, *Norton Puny Pants,*" Snarls called after them, but not too loudly.

CHAPTER 4

MESOGGIE CASTLE

Back at Mesoggie Castle, and after everyone was clean and shiny, the puny chefs brought out an elaborate, if somewhat puny, buffet of mini seaweed tarts, mini soufflés, mini apple strudels, and mini onion juice cocktails. Everyone munched and mingled inside the dining hall. All except Snarls, who was forced to sit his body outside the miniature castle as only his head would fit inside, through the dining hall window. Some of the braver puny knights tried to appease him by offering him puny snacks.

Snarls would just turn his head away and huff out puffs of smoke.

Petra and Norton sat side by side upon Norton's oversized purple throne at the front of the dining hall. "Norton, we have known each other for nearing six new moons now, and it is just perchance I visit your kingdom for the first time while you have visited my kingdom thrice thus far."

"Well, Petra, your kingdom is on higher ground. You have no need to dry out as often as swamp knights do." They both laughed. "And just this very morn, I declared to the puny army that it was near time to visit Kingdom Pen Pieyu to dry out our gear and, of course, ourselves, and all the puny army whooped and hollered, then sealed the deal by throwing beet juice at me."

"Time it is, then. You and the puny army haven't been by since Bograt's knighting party."

"Speaking of, where is Bograt? I thought you told me all knights in your kingdom, well, you and Bograt since you are the only knights of your kingdom, must stick together. Why is she not sticking to you? And what do you mean your visit is perchance?"

Petra chuckled, sighed, then frowned. "Well, first off, Bograt has been detoured by a capturing wave that has taken her on a side-trip adventure. I'm sure she's okay though, and she should find her way back to us soon enough. Secondly, Father has written a new rule in the royal rule book. We are here only because Bograt and I are on a royal-sealed mission to capture the first car-panther encountered in the Kingdom of Boogy Gobees."

With that announcement, Norton turned an odd grey color, and everyone in the room gasped, some dropped their juice glasses while others ran away. Snarls' eyes grew buggy huge; within a two-count, he ripped out a fire stream. The fire stream went over the heads of all the puny army, but caught on Petra's pink plume and toasted it.

"Snarls!" Petra slapped at the fiery commotion on her helmet. "That's the second plume you've ruined in six new moons."

"Yeah, well, sorry, but losing your plume is semi-minor compared to losing half your body," Snarls snapped. "You know what Bograt said, notorious-fabled car-panthers eat dragons! That's scary!"

Petra hurried over to console Snarls by rubbing his nose. "Snarls, I will never let anything happen to you, and you know that Bograt just makes things up. Nobody knows what a car-panther is, remember? I told you that," Petra said, her voice crackling and not sounding as reassuring as she wanted it to.

"Really? Then why are they all so scared?" Snarls motioned with his nose in the direction of Prince Nastybun, his puny army, and the puny chefs. They were all huddling in a quivering ball: some feet up in the air, some arms holding platters of food, and the odd head poking out here and there. They looked like they were about to roll away with the whole party.

Petra forced her voice stronger, "We'll show them, Snarls. We're not scared of a new adventure, right? And one just never knows what is real until one sees it for oneself."

Snarls gave a weak, scrunched-to-the-side grin.

CHAPTER 5

LAND OF THE BOOGY GOBEES

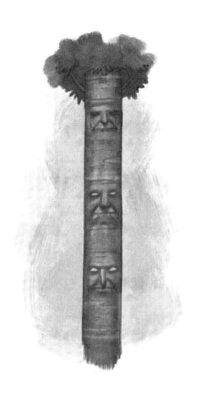

Early the next morning, after a puny breakfast of puny crusty croissants and puny deviled eggs, and then a rushed good-bye to the nail-biting Prince Nastybun and his pale-looking puny army, Snarls and Petra headed east again toward the Kingdom of Boogy Gobees.

"It's good to finally be out of those humid and mucky swamps, right, Snarls?" Petra slid off his back, onto the drier ground.

"I hate mud," Snarls complained and fidgeted while Petra used her bare hands to scoop the biggest mud clumps from between his mud-packed claws. "And if Nastybun had a proper-sized castle with a proper-sized kitchen, I could have whipped us up a real breakfast, say, creamed sargasso on eggs la-dee-da or my broccoli onion-nowhere-to-be-seen dish that you like so much. As it were, we are starved."

As they entered the forest, Snarls darted and flashed his eyes about the shadows. He made quick ducking manoeuvres as if he was dodging something.

"Notice how straight and tall these poplar trees are," Petra said, trying to ease Snarls' anxiety, "like a giant army guarding a kingdom. If I use my good imagination, I can see faces and figures of soldiers in the bark of each tree. And the sparse pine trees look like kings with cloaks on."

"Puhhh," Snarls snorted as they made their way deeper into the forest.

Petra then tried to lighten Snarls' bad mood by singing a ballad that was a favorite amongst Pen Pieyu bards:

Prince Noble from south kingdom afar
Journeys his heart by the light of star
To find his way to the fair Princess True
To pledge his love while returning her shoe
And to make his chivalry perfectly clear
He will offer to fight dragons for his dear.

Petra eyed Snarls. The song definitely did nothing to cheer him. Thinking of what else to do, she bellowed out the song again with her made-up lyrics to replace the last lines:

While he admired his reflection in the mirror
The king's crocodile chair up and bit him on the rear!

"Stop it. You sound like a cat with its tail stuck under a coach wheel," Snarls griped.

"Really?" Petra questioned. "Nobody has ever told me that before."

"Yeah, well, they're just being polite by not saying so," Snarls said, then added, "You know that it takes a true friend to tell you stuff like that, right? You have a great talent for writing and storytelling, and some fairly good knight skills, but singing is not your forte."

"Sure, Snarls, that's good that you told me, I guess." Petra thought about this for a moment. "I never really liked singing lessons anyway—kind of dull. I suppose then I'll stick with storytelling, writing, knight lessons, and highland dancing. I'm pretty good at those things, and that's because I like them better than singing."

"Excellent!" Snarls gushed, just a bit too excited. Then suddenly he vanished.

Petra whirled around twice before slowing to scrutinize every tree soldier; their branches seemingly turning into threatening aiming weapons. She grappled for her sword, swooping low, trying to get a better ground view. Nothing.

Snarls was not there. Nobody, nothing was behind the trees that she could see.

What dark magic lurks here? Where could he be?

In the next moment, she heard her first dragon scream. It made her neck hair stand up, and her legs wanted to run back toward the swamps.

"Aaah haa! *So* horrible!" burst out the cries. "Doomsday, I saaaay!"

Then a different voice, a calmer voice that was obviously chewing while it spoke, "Oh. It's not so bad. A nice sunny day...to just be hanging around in car-panther country, caught up in a car-panther trap."

"*No.* Eeweee!"

"Where are you?" Petra rushed around and between the trees.

"Up heeeere," Snarls wailed.

Petra jerked her head upward. There, confined inside a large net that hung from a bent treetop was Snarls' scrunched up body. And a little over to the right, in a net of her own, was Bograt, who appeared quite relaxed as she munched on onions and cattail stems.

Petra let out a heavy sigh. "Thank the crab gods you are both all right, but how in the entire kingdom did you both get up there?" Petra tried not to giggle as she watched Snarls twist and turn into positions she never thought possible, his head finally popping out between his back legs. "Get me out of here! Hurry! Before the car-panthers come!" Snarls screeched.

"Calm down, you nitwit dragon. The whole of all the kingdoms will hear you. Here, munch on this so you can think straight." Bograt threw him an onion. It hit him on the head.

"Ow!"

"Whoops."

"Snarls, try and use your fire to make a hole in your net. Meanwhile, Bograt, you try to swing toward Snarls and latch onto his net so he can singe a hole in your net and free you. Don't scorch Bograt though."

"Pwaaaah, *snort*, puuugh, *puff*, puuugh. It's…not …working. Oh, what a way to go! Teeth marks so do not suit me."

Petra paced, glancing up and around and down, trying to figure out something that might work. She tried not to dwell upon what Bograt said—that this was car-panther country and most likely car-panther traps, because if they were, surely the car-panthers would be coming around soon.

An idea came to her. "Bograt, I'm going to climb the tree you're hung by. I'll give you my sword. You cut Snarls out, then yourself."

Petra took off her helmet and tossed it to the side. The tree wouldn't be easy to climb—no branches until about twenty feet up, she noticed. She recalled the warm-up exercises she learned in highland dance class where she had to twist her leg inward from the knee, then snap it back to the floor; she decided this would be the best way to grip and climb the tree until she could reach the first branch.

She struggled for grip, slid down more than she climbed up. But little by little, as she realized she had to grip her knees tighter around the back of the tree, the method started to work better. She reached for the first branch. It broke. She nearly lost her balance but grabbed higher and barely caught on to the second branch. The second branch was stronger, holding fast to the tree. She wiggled her way up and then along the branch until she was able to sit full up.

"Bravo!" Snarls cheered out.

"I thought you were scared. Why are you laughing?"

"I am scared, but that was the most ridiculous-looking tree climb I have ever seen."

"Who cares how ridiculous it looks if it works?" Petra said, trying to catch her breath.

She handed Bograt her sword. Bograt rolled her eyes. "You do know that is a cake knife, right? How about I just use my dagger?"

"Seriously, Bograt, you could have just told me that before! Hurry then, cut Snarls loose, then yourself."

Bograt sawed at the net by Snarls' head. Snarls backed away as much as he could, considering his butt was on top of his head. After much effort, one of the strings in the rope snapped, unravelled, and then slapped Snarls in the eye.

"Yeow!" *Paaawoosh*! Out roared a fire streak from Snarls that caught his net on fire, then Bograt's net was aflame. In a blink of an eye, the two of them tumbled out and splattered onto the ground; Bograt splattered more softly as she landed on top of Snarls.

"Ooof," Snarls' breath whooshed out of him as his eyes bugged huge, then fluttered closed.

Petra scurried down the tree, scratching and scraping her own limbs in the process.

"Snarls! Are you all right?" She knelt by Snarls, stroking his mud-crusted brows.

After a few moments, Snarls flipped one eye open. "Sure, yeah, I'm all right. I just fell a bazillion lengths from a tree, out of a car-panther net while a bog witch, who surely weighs fifty stones, pulverized me and then tried to kill me with her onion-breath, and now I see my tail is smoking. Why wouldn't I be all right?"

"Oh, thank the crab gods, Snarls," Petra sang out.

"I'm good too," Bograt added, got up, and brushed off some branches, leaves, and rope parts.

"Yes, yes. I'm so glad to see you, Bograt. I thought we lost you." Petra attempted to hug her, but Bograt scrunched her face, handed over one of the onion sacks that were tied behind her neck, and backed away.

Then another voice, a chirpy crisp voice cut in, "Well, tickle my Friday fancy pants, what do we have here? It looks like a drag-goon, a messy mess person, and quite possibly the Princess Knight."

Petra and Snarls turned toward the voice. "Aaah!" they yelled in unison. Petra grabbed two onions, ready to fire them.

"Good to see you, Bograt," the cheery voice chuckled.

"Hey, Findor, brought you some onions." Bograt grabbed the sack back from Petra and handed both sacks over.

"Excuse me!" Petra snapped as she eyed the lanky greenish creature with the ruby-red smile that stretched across his face. "What and who are you? How do you know I am the Princess Knight? And—"

"Findor Woodrow," he said, stepping forward with his hand extended. "I live here, in the Kingdom of Boogy Gobees. I am an elven carpenter, as are all of the elven that live here."

Bograt sniggered. "Meet the car-panthers."

Snarls jumped backward, covered his mouth, and bit down on his claws.

"You're a car-panther?" Petra squeaked out.

"Car-*pen-ters*. You're saying it wrong. As in carpenters who build things," Findor explained. He turned his grin toward Bograt, and soon enough, the two of them let out a good length of laughter. "And I know about you and your drag-goon friend here because Bograt has enlightened me with her, uh, fond stories."

"Well then," was all Petra could think to say to Findor, then scowled at Bograt with her best you-are-a-menace glare.

"Carpenter. Ha! You are a carpenter, not a car-panther? That is so hilarious," Snarls laughed out while slapping his knee, then arched a suspicious eyebrow. "So what do carpenters eat?"

Findor's grin widened so wide it looked like it might wide-slide right up and off his face. "Well, pitted corkwood, that is a strange question, but to answer, elven kind eat only vegetables."

Snarls blew out a long sigh with traces of sparks riding on his breath. "By the way, I am a dra*gon*, not a drag-*goon*. You're saying it wrong."

"That's funny, Bograt said you were a...oh, never mind. Come, you must be starving. We'll feast at King Hobnobby's castle. That's where we live."

CHAPTER 6

HOBNOBBY CASTLE

As the foursome walked in a staggered row toward King Hobnobby's castle, Petra and Findor dove straight into chatting about all things they had heard of the other's kingdom. Snarls was giving Bograt his squish-eyed glare. Bograt hummed and turned her head the other direction.

"I shouldn't be surprised that you know Bograt," Petra told Findor. "She has the wanderlust for sure."

"Ha. True. Bograt told me you would be coming for a missing, though for a missing what, I do not know."

Petra smiled, then frowned. "I'm on a miss*ion*, not a miss*ing*. And if I don't complete my mission, I will lose my knighthood, as will Bograt."

"Well, that seems a little harsh," Findor said. "What is this mission about?"

"Truth be told, I must capture the first car-panther I encounter to bring back to my kingdom."

Findor made an intense gulping sound. Petra felt her cheeks redden.

They walked in an awkward silence, but Findor didn't run, Petra didn't capture, Snarls didn't breathe fire on anyone, and Bograt was just plain quiet for a change.

Finally, they arrived at the gates of King Hobnobby's castle in the Kingdom of Boogy Gobees. Findor's brows were knitted tight, and his face seemed a lighter shade of green as he guided them through the crooked, misshapen pillars on either side of the mismatched-sized double doors. Once inside, Petra marvelled at the whole of the castle. *It is so completely built wrong,* she thought. The walls on one side were at least ten feet lower than on the other side, and all the walls had lumps with twigs and leaves poking out. The floors appeared to have trip bumps everywhere. Not one of the windows were the same size or at the same level, and some windows were even tilted sideways. Petra thought better than saying anything to Findor since he was a carpenter, and carpenters build things, and Findor had already told her the carpenters lived at Hobnobby Castle.

"Why is everything so crooked? And look at these bumps. Sheesh, what a wacky mess!" Snarls blurted out.

Findor rubbed his hand in circles over a bulge on the wall; this motion seemed to smooth the clay out for a moment before it buckled again. "We are tree-loving carpenters. We do not harm nor hurt tree souls, and therefore, we will not build with wood. Building things with the clay we have here, especially big things like a castle—well, it's just not easy. Everything has a tendency to sag when no wooden cross braces are used, and they sag more each year." Findor gave a long sigh.

Petra moved in closer to stroll down the length of one wall while gliding her hand across the rough surface—again, the wall smoothed only to buckle back up. She rubbed her chin and pondered over Findor's dilemma with the clay castle and the carpenter's conviction to not harm trees. Her thoughts then landed on the importance of trees: how trees purify the air, how decaying trees fertilize the earth, how trees shelter farmers' fields from the winds that would just as soon pick up soil to land it in another kingdom. She smiled at the thought of the beautiful pine, poplar, and spruce forests in her own land that housed faeries, gnomes, western elves, and the ganutes, and how those very trees flourished as their inhabitants nurtured them. Petra snapped out of her daydream and spoke softly, "Findor, you are right to not harm trees. Trees are alive, as alive as any other creature I know. There must be another solution for your castle."

An idea struck her. "Snarls!" she shouted louder than she meant to. Snarls gave a start as did most everyone else. "You know how the royal potters at Longstride Castle have to bake the pottery in the kiln before it is set? That is what needs to be done here—the clay has to be baked before it will hold."

"I don't think there is a kiln big enough—oh, you mean me..." Snarls looked down and shuffled his feet, his cheeks turning a raspberry red.

Petra understood. Snarls' fire didn't work so well. After all, he had accidently blasted her helmet plume to smithereens on more than one occasion; then as he tried to fire-blast Prince Duce Crablips when Duce had threatened them on their way to Talent School, Snarls could only manage to blow out smoky onion peels to cover the prince; and when the king announced Petra's mission to capture a car-panther, he got so excited he fire-blasted the queen's hair. Yes, Snarls had a big problem controlling his fire.

Findor's face lit up a bright green. "Yes, yes, the dragon, by willygads! He can fire-bake the clay and save the castle." Then just as quickly, his cheeriness dimmed down. "You are kind to want to help save

Hobnobby Castle, but we still have a problem: the capturing part, to save your knighthoods. I appreciate what you offer, but I refuse the capturing part, to be thrown into a dungeon to rot like last week's banana bread." Findor squinted one eye. "But if I don't agree to the capture part, will I be put in a frilly dress for interfering in a knight's mission? By wallybots, either way, it's just nasty." Findor started pacing in a circle.

Petra chuckled. The king's rule about putting mission-interfering persons into frilly dresses always got this reaction. It was the most ridiculous rule he ever made, yet somehow, it was the best rule he ever made. But soon enough, the seriousness of the situation caught up to her: either capture Findor or lose her knighthood. Petra joined the same circle path, pacing behind Findor. Without much hesitation, Snarls started up the pace behind her. Bograt whistled and leaned against the wall.

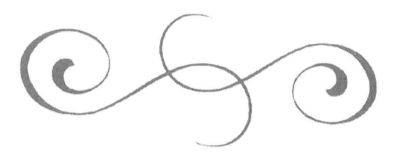

CHAPTER 7

DRAGON FIRE

After many circles with many "Hmmm"s and "Aahha"s coming from the trio, Petra suddenly stopped pacing. Snarls bumped into her; Findo, who had lapped them several times, slammed into Snarls' scaly backside with a "Yeow!"

"Findor, I am through with my shilly-shallying, plus I have decided. I will not capture you. Capturing is wrong and not honorable at all."

"Your knighthood!" Findor and Snarls shouted out in unison.

"Hmm, yes, that is a problem. But you know, I am sure I can get another knighthood if I really try," Petra said, forcing a smile. "Oh, and don't worry about the frilly dress thing. I will tell Father I have failed the mission—that I could not capture a car-panther nor even came across a car-panther that could have interfered with my mission."

Findor's wide mouth fell wide open. Snarls' eyebrows lifted upward until they touched his ears. Bograt snickered and munched on an onion.

"That is...honorable. No, it is so much more so than honorable. It is noble. And the kindest thing ever..." Findor's voice trailed off; he sniffled and wiped a tear that made a whitish track down his cheek.

Snarls cringed a moment, then took a deep breath, and raised his snout high. "I will try to fire-bake your clay castle. It is the least I can do in the wake of what the Princess Knight has just offered."

Petra spread her arms and flattened her body against Snarls' chest. Snarls placed gentle claws around her to hug her back. His shaking did not go unnoticed by her.

"We have work to do then. Findor, gather all the carpenters. Have them smooth out the walls. Snarls, try as hard as you can try to make your fire work. Try, Snarls. You can do it if you really try. I know you can." Petra rubbed him on the soft part at the end of his nose. "You just have to believe in yourself, Snarls. I believe in you."

Snarls looked down at her with eyes full of worry. Petra smiled and nodded up at him.

As per Findor's instructions, the rest of the carpenters hurried about and set straight to work: they slung the rope ladders, gave out trowels, and began the process of smoothing over the lumps in the wall and keeping them smooth while they waited for Snarls.

Snarls twisted his body this way and that, trying on different poses, but he didn't seem happy with any one pose. He scrunched and wiggled his face into different expressions, but those didn't seem to hold fast either. After a long spell of poses, scrunches, and wiggles, he puffed up his chest, took a deep breath, then one more for good measure, and blew. What came out was a weak swirl of steam.

Petra winked at Snarls and started up a chant, "You can do it. Just believe in yourself." She motioned the others to join in the chant.

"You can do it. Just believe in yourself," the voices repeated.

Snarls made a low growling sound, then sucked in a bigger breath, blowing it out with so much force his eyes crossed. A pencil-thin line of fire shot out.

Petra knew Snarls was trying his hardest, trying to please her. It made her heart fall and sing at the same time. She motioned the carpenters to gain momentum in the chant.

"You can do it. Just believe in yourself. You can do it," the voices bellowed out while hands clapped to the rhythm of their words.

Snarls stepped closer to the wall and narrowed his eyes. Without much warning, he blasted out a sure and swift fireball that pounded the wall and spread out like a squid's tentacles. A few of the slower carpenters were caught off guard; those few scurried off while slapping at their butts.

Petra hurried to the wall to help the carpenters smooth. Bograt shrugged and joined in.

It was grueling work for everyone at the wall: constantly smoothing and straightening out the clay, keeping the clay in place until they were sure Snarls was ready to blast the spot, then hightailing out of the way before they got scorched.

Snarls was soaked in sweat beads from the concentration and the heat, but determination still smoldered in his eyes. The whole perfected process went on for many hours, nobody daring to stop and rest for fear the dragon's fire might falter. When darkness fell, all the walls were finished. The carpenters put up the torch lights, and they started on the floor.

CHAPTER 8

THE SECOND KNIGHTING

Morning sunlight tickled Petra's face so as to wake her from her slumber. Snarls, Bograt, Findor, and all the carpenters were sprawled out around her on the newly leveled floor. Gazing around at her friends and the newly formed clay castle, a proud tear fell from her eye.

"Arise, my subjects! Who be the newcomers, and pray tell, who or what is responsible for redecorating my castle?" a thunderous voice bellowed out, startling everyone.

Findor straightened his tunic, hurried to the throne, and gave a deep bow. "King Hobnobby, you have returned from your journey. Welcome home. By willigars, it is swell to see you, sire." He bowed to the king again, then curtsied to Petra. "Sire, this is the Princess Knight of Kingdom Pen Pieyu." With two more curtsies, he said, "Snarls, the dragon, formerly of the Forest of Doom and now of Kingdom Pen Pieyu. And Bograt, the bog witch, formerly of the bogs and now of Kingdom Pen Pieyu too. Sire, they have all helped to save Hobnobby Castle, well, each in their own way. Yes, even Bograt, well, and of course the carpenters present—oh, and some have lost their knighthood, but we have a good stash of onions for winter—"

"Findor, slow down. You are rattling on like a boiling kettle," King Hobnobby said with a good humor about him.

"Well, you see, sire, to put it in a seashell, Snarls has saved Hobnobby Castle by baking the clay with his fire breath. It was the Princess Knight's idea. We all helped too. The castle stands firm forevermore. Is it not wondrous and willy-smacking great?"

King Hobnobby laughed a jovial laugh as he held both sides of his head, which was a much darker green and a much larger-sized head than the heads belonging to the other elven. "It is magnificent! It is wondrous! I am absolutely glorious with hobnobbyish delight!" He became so giddy with giggles, he finally lost his breath altogether; then he fell backward onto his throne. The king motioned Snarls forward.

"Sire, there is more," Findor continued, slower, and with a crackle in his voice, "The Princess Knight was administered a mission by her father, King Longstride of Kingdom Pen Pieyu. The mission is to capture a car-panther, by which he means carpenter, and bring it back to her kingdom."

Gasps erupted from the carpenter audience.

"The Princess Knight has willingly forfeited her mission to capture me, or any carpenter. By her own accord, sire, she has relinquished her knighthood and decided upon Bograt's knighthood also, for both their knighthoods will be lost if she should fail the mission."

King Hobnobby's eyes sparkled with admiration. He stood, propped up his ball of a belly to sit on his wide belt, and made his sword sing as he whipped it out of his scabbard. Nodding toward the Pen Pieyu trio, he held his sword out for the dubbing. They stepped forward. King Hobnobby laid the flat side of his sword on Petra's right shoulder, then on her left shoulder, and said, "I pronounce you, Sir Petra of Kingdom Boogy Gobees." To Snarls, he made the same gestures. "I pronounce you, Sir Snarls of Kingdom Boogy Gobees."

When he motioned toward Bograt, she shrugged and turned away. "Nah," she quipped, "knighthood is not all it's cracked up to be."

Petra and Snarls turned to face the crowd. A multitude of whistles, cheers, and guffaws echoed throughout the castle.

Bograt let loose an onion fly, which missed the two newly knighted knights and whacked King Hobnobby square in the left eye. The carpenters all turned still as stone, their eyes wide in astonishment and anticipation. The king rubbed his eye and groaned.

"Oops," Bograt said. "Maybe not a food-throwing party here?"

"Food-throwing makes for the best knighting parties back home," Snarls piped in.

"You want a food-throwing party? So be it!" King Hobnobby proclaimed with one closed watery eye. He clapped his hands, and instantly food appeared on shiny silver trays brought in by the castle chefs.

Everybody chomped on carrots, tomatoes, kale, broccoli, celery, and the onions that Bograt had brought. Then they threw the half-eaten pieces at each other, ducking and diving as flying food zipped around the room like swarms of bees. Snarls hastily flung a few broccoli pieces toward Petra's head, then beelined after the chefs into the kitchen, pulling out his crumpled resume as he ran.

CHAPTER 9

THE TELLING
OF HOW

When the hullabaloo of the knighting party had wound down, fragments of vegetables lay on top of chaises and chandeliers and in heaps on the floor. The partygoers sat or lay on the floor, winded and out of breath too.

King Hobnobby, still chuckling, plopped onto his throne. He patted the seat of the throne beside him. "Come, sit with me, Sir Petra, and tell me of all things of Kingdom Pen Pieyu."

Petra scooted up on the high throne, and the carpenters gathered around to listen. She told of how her father constantly made new and ridiculous rules in the royal rule book, which, somehow, always led to her next adventure. How she acquired her knighthood and how that led to Snarls becoming her royal steed and best friend. How she met and made friends with Prince Nastybun of Kingdom Mesoggie, then with Prince Duce Crablips of the most southern kingdom, Kingdom of Crablips. How she obtained her writing certificate at Talent School. How she encountered the ganutes of the Vast Wilderness and how that led to Bograt becoming a knight. And finally, how it was they ventured to the Kingdom of Boogy Gobees.

During the whole of her story, many "Ooooh"s and "Aaaah"s and a few "Yikes"s escaped from the elven crowd.

"So you see, King Hobnobby, my father, King Longstride, spends the whole of his time writing silly rules in the royal rule book, trying to deter me from being a knight, trying to make me into a girly princess. And as of late, I will lose my knighthood in the Kingdom of Pen Pieyu, but even so, that will not make me into the princess he desires me to be." Petra thought a moment before adding, "I may have lost my knighthood of Kingdom Pen Pieyu, and one day, I will surely gain it back, but of the most importance is the pride I own by doing what is right and noble, by refusing to capture anyone. Also, I am a knight of Kingdom Boogy Gobees. I am proud of that.

"Fahhh, being a knight of Pen Pieyu is just a bunch of hooey to me," Bograt blurted. "Anyhow, Petra, you're still the official, and quite good I might add, storyteller of Pen Pieyu. King Huffy Pants can't take that away from you."

Petra smiled. Bograt's endearment was not lost on her.

King Hobnobby laughed out loud. "Well, I know not what knight benefits I can bestow upon you other than my sincere gratitude and my lifelong friendship."

Petra hopped off the throne and curtsied to the king. Bograt attempted a curtsy that looked more like a tilt. All the carpenters bowed to their king and to Petra. Snarls, coming out of the kitchen balancing two shiny silver trays of hors d'oeuvres, noticed all the bowing and curtsying and decided best he should do the same. He attempted a bow, fumbled the tray and lost his balance, which led to a burst of fire stream slipping out of him and straight toward the empty throne beside King Hobnobby. The blast instantly torched all what was velvet of the chair, leaving only the framework and a few surviving feathers to flutter to the floor.

Petra bit down on her lip but couldn't contain her giggles. Snarls' eyes grew as big as two full moons, but he snickered nonetheless. Soon the whole kingdom was roaring with laughter, King Hobnobby the loudest of all.

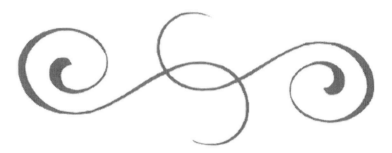

CHAPTER 10

THE RULE ABOUT THE FIRST KNIGHTING

Petra led the trio home by remembering the markings of the way they had previously come. Before long, Bograt spotted a mangy fox she said she knew and had dealings with and went off chasing after him. When the dark fell, a lone wolf howled out his eerie story, which seemed to beckon the owners of thunderous giant wings to overtake the night sky and black out the waning moon. Petra and Snarl tried to ignore the darkness and night noises by reminiscing and laughing about their latest adventure, and somehow, as they kept their good moods about them, the Boogy Gobees Forest became less spooky, as did the swamps and bogs when they came to cross those.

When they approached the torch-lit gates of Longstride Castle, Petra noticed the victory flag flying at full-mast, and music and jovial sounds coming from within. She wondered what the celebration was all about.

Petra and Snarls entered the royal throne room. All eyes turned to them and silence befell the crowd.

"My dear, dear, Princess Petra!" the king shouted out, offering up his upturned palms in welcome. "You have returned."

"Yes, Father." Petra said. "I sense by all the merriment that you have already heard the news then."

"Yes, you have failed your mission, Petra. I understand it is a very sad day for you, but the celebration is about the return of my daughter, *the princess.*" He gave a quick wink to the very-much-so grinning queen.

Petra took a deep breath and straightened tall. "Father, I may have failed your mission, but I have gained something of more value by not capturing a car-panther—I have gained honor. Oh, by the way, you are saying it wrong—they are *carpenters* and now my friends who may one day try to attain knighthood here, which is, as you know, allowed to anyone according to that particular royal-sealed rule in the royal rule book. And some other good news for you, Father. Snarls and I have been granted knighthoods in Kingdom Boogy Gobees." Petra and Snarls smiled and nodded to each other. "Oh, there is one more thing to straighten out…"

With that, the queen flopped her head on the side wing of her chair and squinted her eyes. The king tugged at his grey beard, his suspicious eyes darting back and forth.

Petra held her head higher, then motioned for the royal councilman to approach and to bring the royal rule book with him.

The councilman complied by sliding the book toward her feet. The wide-eyed crowd gasped with squeaks of "Eek"s and "Uh-oh"s. The royal soldiers peeked out of the royal onion room, wondering at the chaos. Bograt sat on her haunch, in the corner, and grinned.

Petra turned to a page in the book and found the spot. "Here, Father. The book says that I must capture a car-panther." She looked him straight in the eye. "There is no such thing as a car-panther."

"Oooooh!" erupted from the crowd, and some juice glasses smashed to the floor.

"A technicality, nothing more than a misplaced hyphen and two wrong letters," the king replied, waving his arm through the air.

"Yes, Father, a technical error, on your part."

Upon understanding the importance of what Petra was saying, the royal councilman scurried over to the royal rule book, grabbed it up, flipped back two pages, and read, "A mission must be a true mission. Nothing can be false about a true mission nor lead to any falsehoods under false pretenses, which would make the true mission false and thus void the true mission to be deemed a false mission." His eyelids fluttered for a spell before he added, "Sire, this means the princess is still a knight here, as is Bograt."

Petra crossed her arms and gave the king her best that-is-right-and-you-know-it look. "And, Father, the next time you write a royal-sealed rule, it would be wise to take your spelling and intention of your words more seriously."

"Oh, just this one more little tiny matter, sire," the royal councilman piped in. "According to your rule about knights of other kingdoms, henceforth the dragon shall be addressed as Sir Snarls."

Promptly, the queen fainted. The king plopped down so hard on his chair that a ball of dust rose up, lingered around his head a moment before it vanished inside his gaping mouth, which caused him to have a sneezing fit and fall off his chair completely.

Petra turned to face the crowd. Snarls scampered over beside her. They clasped hand and claw and bowed toward the royal subjects. The royal councilman gave them each a swift pat on the back.

The crowd raised their glasses of onion juice, clinking glasses together while cheering, whooping, hooting, hollering, and in general, going wild with the excitement of it all. Even Claymore—the royal mastiff—stirred from his never-ending lollygagging and seemed to be grinning. Bograt flung a celery stalk at Petra. Soon thereafter, and without much hesitation at all, food started to fly around the room.

From The Author To Kids And Dragons

Great news for kids and dragons. My next book entitled *The Dragon Grammar Book – Grammar for Kids, Dragons, and the Whole Kingdom* (forthcoming 2017) has absolutely nothing to do with learning grammar.

Well, okay, it does, but it will be a fun way to learn. The Pen Pieyu characters have all agreed to be featured in the example sentences so the lessons will be like reading about them on their adventures. You already know how zany the characters are, so you can expect some hilarious sentences that they come up with all on their own. I hope you will enjoy Petra, Snarls, and the gang as they play with words and those funny marks we call punctuation.

—Diane Mae Robinson

From The Author To The Rest Of The Kingdom

My next book entitled *The Dragon Grammar Book – Grammar for Kids, Dragons, and the Whole Kingdom* (forthcoming 2017) came about because of my own frustrations with looking up grammar rules that didn't seem comprehensible to adults, let alone kids. I decided to break down some of these complicated grammar and writing rules, make them simple and understandable, add in a dash of humor, and let all the characters of The Pen Pieyu Adventures series do the teaching in the example sentences. What has unfolded in this book is an easy-to-understand grammar book that will be fun for kids, adults, and dragons alike, so learning grammar won't be so much like being stuck in a dungeon.

—Diane Mae Robinson

If you enjoyed reading Sir Princess Petra's Mission, reviews are always appreciated by the author. Reviews can be posted on:

Amazon
Barnes & Noble
Goodreads

Sign up for The Dragon Newsletter to receive your free 55-page Sir Princess Petra coloring book:

https://dragonsbook.com/subscribe/

Author website: https://www.dragonsbook.com

Made in the USA
Middletown, DE
20 September 2018